Walt Disney's
MICKEY MOUSE
and the
Great Lot Plot

A GOLDEN BOOK • New York
Western Publishing Company, Inc.
Racine, Wisconsin 53404

"Look at that!" Morty and Ferdie dropped their bat and ball and stared at the sign in front of them.
THE LAND FOR SALE!
"I can't believe it!" said Minnie Mouse. "This is the only vacant lot left for blocks around."

"Maybe whoever buys the land will let children play here," Mickey Mouse said hopefully.

"I'm going to buy it," said a voice behind them. It was Uncle Scrooge McDuck. "It's right next to my money bin, and it's the best place for my new business—SCROOGE'S PERFECTLY PLANTED, PICKED AND PROCESSED, PATENTED PICKLED PRESERVES!"

Morty and Ferdie wrinkled their noses. "Ugh! How can anyone think pickled preserves are more important than baseball?"

But Scrooge was very sure they were. "SCROOGE'S PERFECTLY PLANTED, PICKED AND PROCESSED, PATENTED PICKLED PRESERVES will be a good business," he said. Then he turned and walked away to his money bin.

Mickey and the others followed. They found him
seated on a big pile of money, wiggling his toes
and smiling happily.

"Won't you please think it over, Uncle Scrooge?"
Mickey asked. "The children really need a place to
run and play."

"No!" answered Uncle Scrooge. "My mind is made
up, and that's final!"

"But playgrounds are important!" insisted Mickey. Then, before he quite knew what he was saying, he had made an announcement of his own. "*I'm* going to buy the lot, and I'll make it into a playground for everyone to enjoy."

Scrooge laughed so hard he rolled off the pile of money. "Where will *you* get the money to buy this lot?" he demanded.

As they left the money bin, Mickey's brave smile changed to a frown. "Where *will* I get the money?" he wondered.

But Minnie and the boys were bubbling with excitement. "Why, we'll earn it!" they exclaimed. "Don't worry, Mickey. Our friends will be happy to help, too!"

And so they were! Those next few weeks, Mickey's friends were the busiest people in town. Busiest of all was Mickey himself.

He helped Donald Duck and his nephews wash cars. (Then he helped dry Huey, Dewey, and Louie, who got as wet as the cars they were washing.)

He helped Goofy, whose dog-walking job became too much for him to handle alone.

He helped Morty and Ferdie sell the pies and cakes that Minnie and Daisy Duck baked.

At the end of the month, Mickey counted up all the money that everyone had earned and given to him. It came to exactly five hundred dollars. That wasn't much, and Mickey was worried!

The next day he went to see Uncle Scrooge. "I'm very sad," he said. "All together, we've only been able to earn five hundred dollars, Uncle Scrooge, and I know that isn't enough money to buy the lot. *You* certainly can pay much more than that for it."

"Too bad, Mickey," Uncle Scrooge said, smiling. "Looks like the lot will be mine. It's sure a perfect place for my new pickled preserve factory."

Later that day, Scrooge walked happily down the street and stopped in front of the empty lot.

"Hi, Uncle Scrooge." There were Morty and Ferdie. "Got any jobs you want done?"

"Certainly not!" snapped Uncle Scrooge. "The only help I need is in understanding what's so important about a playground. A lot of foolishness, if you ask me. Humph!"

"We can't tell you—" said Morty.

"But we can show you," added Ferdie.

"Here, catch!" Morty shouted.

And before he knew it, Uncle Scrooge was out on the empty lot, playing a fast game of baseball.

It was nearly dark when the three finally sat
down to rest.

"Well, Uncle Scrooge," said Morty, "now do you
see what's so great about a playground?"

Uncle Scrooge was puffing so hard he couldn't
answer them.

The next day, the boys were waiting when Uncle Scrooge came down the street.

"Tag!" shouted Morty.

"You're it!" yelled Ferdie.

And before he knew what had happened, Uncle Scrooge was chasing the boys across the field.

"You can play all kinds of good games on a playground," said Morty when they stopped to rest at last.

"Humph!" Uncle Scrooge humphed. This time he was so tired that he fell asleep right there under a tree, and while he slept, he had a very strange dream. It was like no dream Uncle Scrooge had ever had before.

The next day, Mickey and his friends watched as the owner of the land put up a new sign on the lot. It said: SOLD TO SCROOGE McDUCK.

Everyone groaned—everyone, that is, except Scrooge. He was overjoyed.

As they all turned to leave, their faces sad, Scrooge shouted, "Wait here a few minutes. I have a surprise for you all!"

Soon workmen began to arrive. They lifted swings and slides into place! They started to dig a swimming pool! In the corner, they marked the lines for a base-ball diamond!

Scrooge just stood there and grinned, while Mickey
and his friends gave three tremendous cheers.

"Uncle Scrooge," Mickey asked, "how can we ever
thank you enough? We're awfully glad you changed
your mind! Now we can buy *uniforms* for all of the
baseball team using our five hundred dollars!"

The day of the first game in the new park finally

arrived. Uncle Scrooge was given the honor of hitting the very first pitched ball.

"Hurrah!" the crowd cheered as the ball soared into the air.

The cheer was cut short by the tinkling of glass. The ball had crashed through a window in Scrooge's own money bin!

"Oh, oh! Sorry about your window, Uncle Scrooge,"
called Mickey.

But Uncle Scrooge was already on his way to first
base. "It's only glass," he shouted over his shoulder.
"But did you see that? I do believe I hit a home run!"